THIS BOOK BELONGS TO

*Dedicated to Fr. Joseph Tedesco
for having the vision to bring us together
to create this book.*

Lisa Suhay would like to thank her sons Zoltan, age seven; Ian, age six; and Avery, age two, for reminding their mother how important it is to keep believing. The author is also grateful to Deepak Chopra and Carolyn Rangel for participating in the Synchrodestiny of this book.

Louis S. Glanzman would like to thank his grandchildren, Trisha, Michelle, Jason, Doug, Jo Ann, Alfred, Katie, Erik, and Evan, and great-grandson, Matthew, for inspiring this work.

The publisher wishes to recognize the gifted Carol Talley for her inspired guidance of all the MarshMedia books.

And special thanks from us all to Susan Schilling . . . so committed to bringing good people together to make great books.

Text © 2001 by Lisa Suhay

Illustrations © 2001 by Louis S. Glanzman

Published by **MARSH**media

A Division of Marsh Film Enterprises, Inc.

P. O. Box 8082

Shawnee Mission, KS 66208

**Library of Congress Cataloging-in-Publication Data**
Suhay, Lisa, 1965–
    Dream catchers / written by Lisa Suhay; illustrated by Louis S. Glanzman.
        p. cm.
    Summary: Inspired by their grandfather and his paintings, a young boy
and girl take an imaginary journey into the distant past, to places of which
they've only dreamed.
    ISBN 1-55942-181-9
    [1. Imagination—Fiction. 2. Art—Fiction. 3. Travel—Fiction. 4. Grandfathers—
Fiction. 5. Dreams—Fiction.]
I. Glanzman, Louis S., 1922– ill. II. Title.
PZ7.S9443Dr 2001
[Fic]—dc21                                            2001030663

*Book layout and typography by Cirrus Design*

Printed in Hong Kong

# DREAM CATCHERS

*Written by* Lisa Suhay

*Illustrated by* Louis S. Glanzman

MarshMedia, Kansas City, Missouri

Zachary and Carolyn had spent too much time watching television. Or so their parents thought.

"What you need is time away from the electric buzz," said their father. "You need to take your minds traveling."

Usually this was Father's way of telling them to go read a book, so Zachary and Carolyn were surprised to learn that they were going to visit their grandfather for the afternoon.

Grandfather was a painter, and an adventure always waited in his sunny studio.

Mother kissed them both and said, "I wonder what Grandfather has in store for you two today."

Zachary and Carolyn found Grandfather in his studio, sitting beside a huge painting.

Zachary could not take his eyes away from the painting. It seemed alive.

Carolyn also felt a strange sort of pull. For just a moment, a blink, she was sure she heard a sound come from the painting.

A knowing look came over Grandfather's face, and his eyes glittered like sun on the water.

"Did it speak to you?" he asked. "People say a painting can speak to you. Of course, we artists know the truth—a painting can really move you."

Zachary was still staring at the painting. "I feel like I could just step into this one and go," he said.

"So you will," Grandfather said. Now he had their full attention.

"Yes," said Grandfather. "Didn't you know that art can take you places?" Then Grandfather gave each a blank scrap of canvas, just like the canvas that he used. "These are your tools. Hold them up and look at them. Picture a place and off you go."

Zachary and Carolyn looked confused.

"I'll start you off," he said. "Like training wheels on a bike. Stand in front of this painting. Look at it closely. See every shade and color, every brush stroke. Now," said Grandfather, "look at your own piece of canvas and see the picture there."

Carolyn and Zachary did just as Grandfather said. They stared at their pieces of canvas, and—sure enough—they saw the picture. And then they saw something more. They saw themselves in the picture!

From far away they seemed to hear Grandfather say, "Go where you dream and dream wherever you go."

And so they did.

Standing in the hot sun and squinting, they spun around and looked for Grandfather, but his studio was gone, and instead of his voice they heard the trumpet and roar of — what was it?

"Triceratops!" Carolyn shouted.

"Let's go pet one!" Zachary said.

"Don't you know anything?" Carolyn cried. "You could be smushed! Eaten!"

Their argument came to a standstill as the sky went dark. Looking up they saw a giant beast, its belly right over their heads.

"Diplodocus!" Carolyn said breathlessly. "It's going to squish us like ants!"

Zachary had an idea. "Wait a minute. This is *our* dream on canvas. We can imagine anything we want!"

"Hmmmmmmm," said Carolyn. "You mean we can imagine that we are invisible to these dinosaurs?"

"Why not?" laughed Zachary.

Now Carolyn had an idea.

"In that case," she said, "let's really take the dino by the horns and ride one."

As soon as the picture of being aboard the Triceratops was in their minds, Zachary and Carolyn found themselves riding high.

With those big horns to hang on to, the Triceratops was perfect for the job.

With the great beast galumphing beneath them, they towered over everything and saw the world from a dinosaur's-eye view.

The ride came to a sudden end when the Triceratops shook them off like fleas. They toppled to the dirt.

"That was fabulous!" said Carolyn, waving her scrap of canvas. "Where to next?"

They had to agree on the place. It would never do for one to shoot off to the moon while the other popped off to a boat on the ocean.

"Cave people," said Zachary with a grin. "Let's change the picture to prehistoric times and visit the cave people. Remember that book at home that tells all about them? Imagine that, and we'll be sure to go straight to the Stone Age."

They held up their scraps of canvas and looked and looked until they called to mind the pictures in their book. Everything around them winked.

The dinosaurs were gone, and in their place were girls and boys and mothers and fathers, having a big meeting around the mouth of a cave. A hairy man waved his arms and grunted. He seemed to be telling an exciting story.

"Can you understand what he's saying?" Carolyn asked.

"Of course not," said Zachary. "He's speaking Stone Age."

Zachary jumped up and down and waved his hat in the air, but the cave people just kept on with their storytelling party.

"Our imaginations are working!" said Carolyn.

Zachary and Carolyn made their way through the crowd and into the cave. There they saw a man holding a stick with some gooey clay on it. They watched him draw on the cave wall—animals and hunters with spears and arrows. He seemed to be telling a story, too—in pictures.

"Father would never let me draw on walls like that," Zachary said. "I'm going to like this place." He reached to pick up a stick, but it slipped right through his fingers, and the man kept on painting.

The cave drawings gave Carolyn a new idea.

"Remember that painting on Grandfather's wall, the one made on deer skin? Remember those hunters on horses and the buffalo? Let's go there!"

Zachary really liked that idea. Out came the scraps of canvas and their dreams, and off they went in a dash of color.

"It's a stampede!" Zachary cried. He and Carolyn had landed in the middle of a herd of running buffalo and galloping horses.

"Maybe this wasn't such a brilliant idea after all!" Zachary shouted.

"Help!" Carolyn cried.

"Look! Hunters!" called Zachary.

"Over here!" called Carolyn. "Help!"

Quick as a blink Carolyn was snatched up by big strong arms and pulled up behind a rider. Zachary found the same happening to him. Unfortunately, they were shaken so hard on the ride that their scraps of canvas fluttered away in the dust.

It was not long before they found themselves carried far from the thundering herd to a clearing. There they were dropped gently to the ground.

"Welcome, Dream Catchers," said one of the riders as the others gathered around. Carolyn and Zachary recognized them from Grandfather's painting.

"Dream Catchers?" said Zachary.

"We welcome you whom we call Dream Catchers—ones who follow their thoughts to new places," said another rider.

"Thank you," answered Carolyn.

"Wait a minute!" said Zachary. "Our canvas pieces are gone. How will we get home again?"

"Be not afraid," said the rider. "We are those who believe in the power of dreams. Our thoughts take us places."

"But we need the canvas," Zachary insisted.

"Come," said the rider and led them to the bank of the nearby river where a woman carried a strange and beautiful basket on her back.

"This is Amani and she will take you in her bull-boat to the one who can help you," he said. "Go with her and ask *our* powerful Dream Catcher how to solve your problem."

The children got in the boat, a little nervous about how safe it might be. Amani smiled at them as she guided the craft to the opposite shore.

"What a wonderful boat," Carolyn said.

"We have lived by water for many lifetimes," the woman said. "Our boats have been made this way for generations. They began as a dream in one person's mind, the kind of dream that comes by day. You call them ideas. Then the dreamer woke and crafted our first boat."

The boat landed at the heart of the busy village. There Carolyn and Zachary were greeted by the chief and welcomed as the new Dream Catchers, who had appeared during the great hunt.

"Because you have come to us during our hunt and we have done so well, we would like to give you whatever will bring you joy," said the chief.

Zachary was eyeing the bows and arrows with a gleam in his eye, but Carolyn spoke first. "We want to see your Dream Catcher." Suddenly remembering her manners, she added, "Please."

"Very well," said the chief.

The man who stepped forward from the crowd seemed familiar. Carolyn and Zachary looked at him very hard. "Grandfather?" they gasped. "You're the Dream Catcher?"

Grandfather smiled, took their hands, and led them to the water's edge.

"So," he said, "you are ready to go home now. Well, that should not be difficult. You don't really need those scraps of canvas to let your imaginations roam, you know."

The three of them pushed through the rushes that grew at the edge of the lake and leaned over.

"Picturing your dreams," said Grandfather, "can be as simple as seeing your reflection in the water. Then choose your own way to catch your dreams. Artists catch their dreams in paint and clay. Architects use steel and stone. Writers catch their dreams in words."

Then he stood up, reached into his vest, and drew out a piece of animal skin. When he unrolled it, the children saw a painting of themselves and their grandfather in his studio, looking at a painting.

Then the chief lifted his arms and said in a voice that sounded like a song:
I dream you and you dream me,
Places gone and yet to be.
All our thoughts have power and might.
Now you have Dream Catcher sight.

And so it was that Carolyn and Zachary found themselves back in Grandfather's studio.

"Didn't I tell you that art can take you places?" chuckled Grandfather. "Now just imagine how exciting your lives as Dream Catchers will be."

"Yes!" said Carolyn and Zachary, dancing with joy.

"Just jump in a dream and go!"

## Illustrated Books for Children From MarshMedia

**Amazing Mallika**
Written by Jami Parkison
Illustrated by Itoko Maeno

**Bailey's Birthday**
Written by Elizabeth Happy
Illustrated by Andra Chase

**Bastet**
Written by Linda Talley
Illustrated by Itoko Maeno

**Bea's Own Good**
Written by Linda Talley
Illustrated by Andra Chase

**Clarissa**
Written by Carol Talley
Illustrated by Itoko Maeno

**Dream Catchers**
Written by Lisa Suhay
Illustrated by Louis S. Glanzman

**Emily Breaks Free**
Written by Linda Talley
Illustrated by Andra Chase

**Feathers at Las Flores**
Written by Linda Talley
Illustrated by Andra Chase

**Following Isabella**
Written by Linda Talley
Illustrated by Andra Chase

**Gumbo Goes Downtown**
Written by Carol Talley
Illustrated by Itoko Maeno

**Hana's Year**
Written by Carol Talley
Illustrated by Itoko Maeno

**Inger's Promise**
Written by Jami Parkison
Illustrated by Andra Chase

**Jackson's Plan**
Written by Linda Talley
Illustrated by Andra Chase

**Jomo and Mata**
Written by Alyssa Chase
Illustrated by Andra Chase

**Kiki and the Cuckoo**
Written by Elizabeth Happy
Illustrated by Andra Chase

**Kylie's Concert**
Written by Patty Sheehan
Illustrated by Itoko Maeno

**Molly's Magic**
Written by Penelope Colville Paine
Illustrated by Itoko Maeno

**Papa Piccolo**
Written by Carol Talley
Illustrated by Itoko Maeno

**Pequeña the Burro**
Written by Jami Parkison
Illustrated by Itoko Maeno

**Plato's Journey**
Written by Linda Talley
Illustrated by Itoko Maeno

**Tessa on Her Own**
Written by Alyssa Chase
Illustrated by Itoko Maeno

**Thank You, Meiling**
Written by Linda Talley
Illustrated by Itoko Maeno

**Toad in Town**
Written by Linda Talley
Illustrated by Itoko Maeno

All are available direct from the publisher or through bookstores. To place an order or to receive a catalog, contact

MarshMedia
8025 Ward Parkway Plaza
Kansas City, MO 64114
(800) 821-3303   FAX (816) 333-7421
www.marshmedia.com

## About the Author

Lisa Suhay is a columnist and news correspondent for the *New York Times* and the author of *Tell Me a Story* and *Tell Me Another Story,* collections of original fables and parables. During the past decade, the concerns of her writing have ranged over issues of social justice, family harmony, and the life of the spirit. *Dream Catchers* is her first illustrated children's book. After five years living with her family aboard a thirty-eight-foot sailboat, Mrs. Suhay, her husband, and their three sons now reside on dry land in Medford, New Jersey.

## About the Illustrator

For more than five decades, the art of Louis Glanzman has graced our coffee tables and bookshelves. His work has captured the events of our history for the covers of the *Saturday Evening Post, National Geographic,* and *Time* magazine, and his images of leaders and heroes past and present hang in the National Portrait Gallery and in public buildings across the United States. He is perhaps most fondly known, however, as the man who brought to life the red-headed heroine of *Pippi Longstocking,* included on *School Library Journal's* list of "One Hundred Books That Shaped the Century." Now from the brush of Louis Glanzman come Carolyn and Zachary, two new heroes, to greet young readers of the twenty-first century. Born in Baltimore, Maryland, Mr. Glanzman and his wife Fran lived on Long Island, New York, for most of his working life before settling in his current home in Medford, New Jersey.

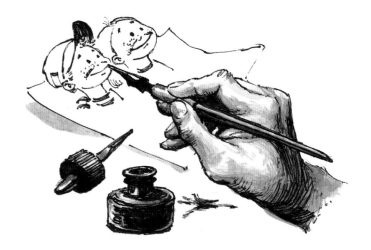